Lion

Bobcat

Panther

Tiger

Puma

Jaguar

Cheetah

Persian cat

Dedicated to all the cats in my life

Eric Carle **Have you seen my cat?**

Aladdin Paperbacks

Have you seen my cat?

This is not my cat!

Have you seen my cat?

This is <u>not</u> <u>my</u> <u>cat</u>!

Have you seen my cat?

This is not <u>my</u> cat!

Have you seen
my cat?

This is not <u>my</u> cat!

This is not <u>my</u> cat!

Have you seen my cat?

This is not my cat!

Have you seen my cat?

This is not <u>my</u> cat!

Have you seen my cat?

This is not <u>my</u> cat!

where is my cat?

Have you seen my cat?

This is my cat!

25 Years of Magical Reading

ALADDIN PAPERBACKS
EST. 1972

First Aladdin Paperbacks edition September 1997
Copyright © 1987 by Eric Carle Corp.
Aladdin Paperbacks
An imprint of Simon & Schuster
Children's Publishing Division
1230 Avenue of the Americas
New York, NY 10020
Also available in a Simon & Schuster Books for Young Readers edition.
Printed and bound in the United States of America
10   9   8   7   6   5   4   3   2   1

The Library of Congress has cataloged the hardcover edition as follows:
Carle, Eric.
Have you seen my cat?
Originally published: New York: F. Watts, 1973.
Summary: A young boy encounters all sorts of cats while searching for the one he lost.
(1. Cats—Fiction.   2. Picture books)   I. Title.
PZ7.C21476Hav   1987   (E)   87-15262
ISBN 0-88708-054-5
ISBN 0-689-81731-2 (Aladdin pbk.)

Lion

Bobcat

Panther

Tiger